# Violin Exam Pieces
## ABRSM Grade 1
Selected from the 2020–2023 syllabus

Name

GW00371041

Date of exam

CD

Violin & Piano  Piano only

## Contents

Violin consultant: Kathy Blackwell
Footnotes: Anthony Burton

---

**Other pieces for Grade 1**   DUET *with violin accompaniment*   PF/VN *with piano or violin accompaniment*

LIST A

**4**  **Arbeau**  Mattachins, arr. Huws Jones. *Encore Violin, Book 1* (ABRSM)

**5**  **Kathy & David Blackwell**  Patrick's Reel. *Fiddle Time Joggers* (OUP)  PF/VN

**6**  **Carse**  Minuet: from *The Fiddler's Nursery for Violin* (Stainer & Bell)

**7**  **Thomas Gregory**  Sinfonia. *Vamoosh Violin, Book 1.5* (Vamoosh)  PF/VN

**8**  **Purcell**  Rigadoon, arr. Nelson (*with repeat*). *Piece by Piece 1 for Violin* (Boosey & Hawkes)

**9**  **Suzuki**  Andantino. *Suzuki Violin School, Vol. 1* (Alfred)  PF/VN

**10**  **Trad. Irish**  John Ryan's Polka, arr. Huws Jones. *Violin Star 2* (ABRSM)  PF/VN

LIST B

**4**  **Kathy & David Blackwell**  Rocking Horse. *Fiddle Time Joggers* (OUP)  PF/VN

**5**  **Katherine & Hugh Colledge**  Full Moon: No. 22 from *Waggon Wheels for Violin* (Boosey & Hawkes)

**6**  **Lehár**  Waltz (from *The Merry Widow*), arr. Huws Jones. *Going Solo for Violin* (Faber) or *The Best of Grade 1 Violin* (Faber)

**7**  **Rodgers & Hammerstein**  Edelweiss (from *The Sound of Music*), arr. Davey, Hussey & Sebba. *Abracadabra Violin (Third Edition)* (Collins Music)  PF/VN

**8**  **Schubert**  Cradle Song, arr. Nelson (*upper part*). *Tunes You Know 1 for Violin Duet* (Boosey & Hawkes)  DUET

**9**  **Trad.**  The Leaving of Liverpool, arr. Huws Jones (*violin melody*). *The Seafaring Fiddler* (Boosey & Hawkes)  PF/VN

**10**  **Trad. English**  A North Country Lass, arr. Huws Jones. *Violin Star 2* (ABRSM)  PF/VN

LIST C

**4**  **Klaus Badelt & Hans Zimmer**  He's a Pirate (from *Pirates of the Caribbean: The Curse of the Black Pearl*), arr. Galliford & Neuburg (*with repeat; ending 1st beat of b. 22*). *Top Hits from TV, Movies & Musicals for Violin* (Alfred)

**5**  **Thomas Gregory**  Fiery Fiddler (*with repeats*). *Vamoosh Violin, Book 1* (Vamoosh)

**6**  **Edward Huws Jones**  Sharks. *Going Solo for Violin* (Faber) or *The Best of Grade 1 Violin* (Faber)

**7**  **Trad. American**  Pick a Bale of Cotton, arr. K. & D. Blackwell. *Fiddle Time Runners* (OUP)  PF/VN

**8**  **Trad. American**  Turkey in the Straw, arr. Cohen & Spearing (*swung rhythm optional*). *Superstart Violin* (Faber)

**9**  **Trad. Chinese**  Jasmine Flower (No. 4), arr. O'Leary. No. 4 from *80 Graded Studies for Violin, Book 1* (Faber)  SOLO

**10**  **Trad. Czech**  Rocking, arr. Nelson (*upper part*). *Tunes You Know 1 for Violin Duet* (Boosey & Hawkes)  DUET

---

First published in 2019 by ABRSM (Publishing) Ltd,
a wholly owned subsidiary of ABRSM, 4 London Wall Place,
London EC2Y 5AU, United Kingdom
© 2019 by The Associated Board of the Royal Schools of Music
Distributed worldwide by Oxford University Press

**Unauthorised photocopying is illegal**
All rights reserved. No part of this publication
may be reproduced, recorded or transmitted
in any form or by any means without the
prior permission of the copyright owner.

Music origination by Julia Bovee
Cover by Kate Benjamin & Andy Potts, with thanks to Brighton College
Printed in England by Halstan & Co. Ltd, Amersham, Bucks.,
on materials from sustainable sources.

# German Dance

No. 8 from 12 German Dances, Hob. IX:10

Arranged by Lionel Salter

Joseph Haydn
(1732–1809)

The German Dance was a well-known 18th-century dance in quick triple time, a forerunner of the waltz. This example comes from a set of 12 such dances published in 1793, which were said to be by the Austrian composer Joseph Haydn, but which are actually based on melodies from an opera by the Spanish composer Vicente Martín y Soler.

© 2019 by The Associated Board of the Royal Schools of Music
Adapted from *Violin Exam Pieces 1993–1994*, Grade 1, arranged by Lionel Salter (ABRSM)

It is **illegal** to make unauthorised copies of this copyright music.

It is illegal to make unauthorised copies of this copyright music.

The New Harp

# Y Delyn Newydd

Arranged by David Blackwell

Trad. Welsh

'Y Delyn Newydd' is Welsh for 'The new harp': the harp is the national instrument of Wales. This piece is a traditional dance tune in the rhythm of the polka, a dance of central European origin which enjoyed worldwide popularity in the 19th century.

© 2019 by The Associated Board of the Royal Schools of Music

It is **illegal** to make unauthorised copies of this copyright music.

A:3

# Hornpipe

No. 2 from *Little Suite No. 3*

Peter Martin
(born 1956)

The hornpipe was a lively dance popular in England from the 16th to 18th centuries, and often considered to be a dance of sailors. There are examples in several different rhythms. This piece by Peter Martin recalls the well-known traditional tune called 'Jack's the Lad', 'The College Hornpipe' or 'The Sailors' Hornpipe'. Peter Martin is a violinist and former string teacher based in the north of England, who now concentrates on composing. Although the composer's metronome mark is ♩ = 132, students may prefer a slower tempo, for example ♩ = *c*.126.

© Copyright 1984 Stainer & Bell Ltd, 23 Gruneisen Road, London N3 1DZ, UK. www.stainer.co.uk
Reprinted by permission. All rights reserved.

It is illegal to make unauthorised copies of this copyright music.

# Round Dance

No. 17 from *For Children*, Vol. 1

B:1

Arranged by Hywel Davies

Béla Bartók
(1881–1945)

*For Children* by the leading Hungarian composer and pianist Béla Bartók is a collection, written in 1908/09, containing 85 easy piano pieces across four volumes. Bartók believed strongly in the 'musical value' of folk melodies: so he chose to base the pieces on Hungarian and Slovak folk song and dance tunes, which he and his friend Zoltán Kodály had recently collected on trips to country villages. The 'Round Dance', here arranged for violin and piano, is a wedding song and dance.

© Copyright 2018 by Boosey & Hawkes Music Publishers Ltd
Reproduced by permission.

It is **illegal** to make unauthorised copies of this copyright music.

B:2

# Ode to Joy

from Symphony No. 9, Op. 125, fourth movement

Arranged by Nicholas Scott-Burt

Ludwig van Beethoven
(1770–1827)

The last of the nine symphonies by the great German composer Ludwig van Beethoven, completed in 1824 and first performed in 1826, did something entirely new: it added solo voices and chorus to the orchestra in its final movement. This finale is a sequence of free variations on a strikingly simple theme; its text is an 'Ode to Joy' by the German poet Friedrich Schiller. The first two verses, sung to the theme, are in praise of the emotion of joy, and the way it encourages belief in the fellowship of humankind.

© 2019 by The Associated Board of the Royal Schools of Music

It is **illegal** to make unauthorised copies of this copyright music.

# Skye Boat Song

B:3

Arranged by Peter Gritton

Trad. Scottish
Collected and adapted by Annie MacLeod
(1855–1921)

The 'Skye Boat Song' is a lullaby for Bonnie Prince Charlie, the 'Young Pretender' to the British throne, as he is rowed to the Isle of Skye following the collapse of his army's invasion of Scotland at the Battle of Culloden in 1746. However, the song dates from much later than that, having been published in 1884. The words were written by Sir Harold Boulton, and the tune was adapted by Annie MacLeod from a traditional Scottish rowing song. The rhythm of the melody suggests the gentle movement of the rowers' oars.

© 2019 by The Associated Board of the Royal Schools of Music

It is **illegal** to make unauthorised copies of this copyright music.

# Tango

No. 2 from *Four Modern Dance Tunes*

Neil Mackay
(1922–1973)

The tango is the national dance of Argentina and is known for its syncopated rhythms (such as the figure in bar 5, first and second beats) and passionate expression. This tango is by Neil Mackay, a British specialist in writing for young violinists and violists. It is the second piece in his collection of *Four Modern Dance Tunes*, published in 1964.

© Copyright 1964 Stainer & Bell Ltd, 23 Gruneisen Road, London N3 1DZ, UK. www.stainer.co.uk
Reprinted by permission. All rights reserved.

It is **illegal** to make unauthorised copies of this copyright music.

# What shall we do with the drunken sailor?

Arranged by Alan Bullard

Trad.

'What shall we do with the drunken sailor?' is a traditional American and British sea shanty, a work song sung by sailors as they haul on ropes or carry out other heavy tasks. While the question asked in the title and in the verse (three times in bars 5–10) is answered with a series of punishments, the words of the chorus (from bar 13) are:

Hooray and up she rises,
Hooray and up she rises,
Hooray and up she rises,
Early in the morning.

© 2019 by The Associated Board of the Royal Schools of Music

It is **illegal** to make unauthorised copies of this copyright music.

C:3

# Chitty Chitty Bang Bang

from *Chitty Chitty Bang Bang*

Arranged by Nikki Iles

Robert Sherman (1925–2012)
and Richard Sherman (born 1928)

*Chitty Chitty Bang Bang* is a 1968 musical fantasy film, based on a novel by Ian Fleming. The title is the name given to an old former racing car, looked after by two children and their inventor father, which in the course of various adventures gains the ability to sail and fly. The name imitates the sounds made by the car in motion. This song, sung affectionately to the car, was written by the American brothers Robert B. Sherman and Richard M. Sherman and has been arranged here by the jazz pianist and educator Nikki Iles.

© Copyright 1968 EMI Unart Catalog Inc.  EMI United Partnership Limited
This arrangement © Copyright 2018 EMI Unart Catalog Inc.
Print rights in Europe administered by Hal Leonard Europe Ltd. Print rights outside Europe administered by Alfred Music. All rights reserved. International copyright secured. Used by permission.